The Flautist's Collection

Book One

Selected & Edited by
Paul Edmund-Davies

Kevin Mayhew

We hope you enjoy *The Flautist's Collection Book 1*.
Further copies of this and the other books in the series are available
from your local music shop.

In case of difficulty, please contact the publisher direct:

The Sales Department
KEVIN MAYHEW LTD
Rattlesden
Bury St Edmunds
Suffolk IP30 0SZ

Phone 01449 737978
Fax 01449 737834

Front Cover: *Willy Lott's House* by John Constable (1776-1837).
Reproduced by courtesy of the Board of Trustees of the
Victoria & Albert Museum, London.

Cover designed by Juliette Clarke and Graham Johnstone.
Picture Research: Jane Rayson.

First published in Great Britain in 1993 by Kevin Mayhew Ltd.

© Copyright 1993 Kevin Mayhew Ltd.

ISBN 0 86209 268 X
Catalogue No: 3611016

All or part of these pieces have been edited by Paul Edmund-Davies
and are the copyright of Kevin Mayhew Ltd.

Series Music Editor: Anthea Smith.

Printed and bound in Great Britain.

Contents

		Page	
		Score	Part
Adagio and Allegro from Sonata in E minor	Johann Sebastian Bach	5	1
Allegretto	Benjamin Godard	24	8
Andantino from Fantasie	Gabriel Fauré	46	16
Allegro from Sonata in C	Wolfgang Amadeus Mozart	39	14
Andante Pastoral	Paul Taffanel	14	4
Aria	Albert Roussel	35	13
Larghetto and Gavotte from Sonata in C	George Frideric Handel	19	6
Sonata in F	Georg Philipp Telemann	28	10
Syrinx	Claude Debussy	34	12

PAUL EDMUND-DAVIES, who selected and edited the music in this book, is the Principal Flautist of the London Symphony Orchestra and has performed as Guest Principal with several other London orchestras. In addition to performing concerti with both the LSO and the English Chamber Orchestra, he has regularly appeared on recordings in both orchestral and solo roles with the Academy of St. Martin-in-the-Fields. He has also made numerous radio and television broadcasts.

ADAGIO and ALLEGRO
from Sonata in E minor
Johann Sebastian Bach (1685-1750)

1. Adagio

Adagio ma non tanto

Keyboard realisation by Colin Hand.

2. Allegro

ANDANTE PASTORAL

Paul Taffanel (1844-1908)

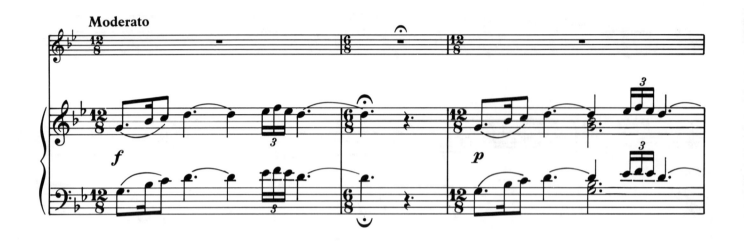

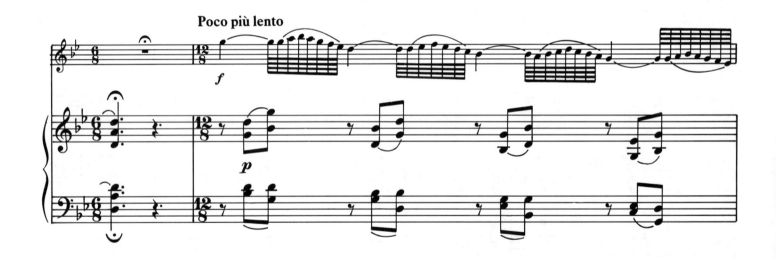

17

LARGHETTO and GAVOTTE
from Sonata in C
George Frideric Handel (1685-1759)

Keyboard realisation by Colin Hand.

Adagio

Tempo di Gavotti

ALLEGRETTO

Benjamin Godard (1849-1895)

The Flautist's Collection

Book One : Selected & Edited by Paul Edmund-Davies

ADAGIO and ALLEGRO

from Sonata in E minor

Johann Sebastian Bach (1685-1750)

2. Allegro

2

ANDANTE PASTORAL

Paul Taffanel (1844-1908)

5

LARGHETTO and GAVOTTE
from Sonata in C
George Frideric Handel (1685-1759)

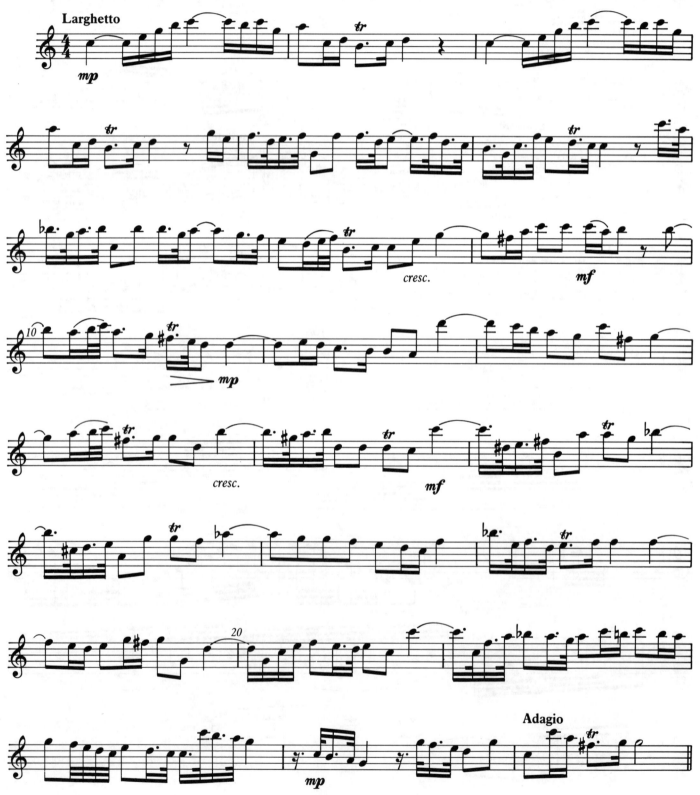

ALLEGRETTO

Benjamin Godard (1849-1895)

SONATA IN F
Georg Philipp Telemann (1681-1767)

1. Vivace

2. Largo

3. Allegro

SYRINX

Claude Debussy (1862-1918)

ARIA

Albert Roussel (1869-1937)

13

ALLEGRO from Sonata in C

Wolfgang Amadeus Mozart (1756-1791)

ANDANTINO from FANTASIE

Gabriel Fauré (1845-1924)

25

SONATA IN F
Georg Philipp Telemann (1681-1767)

1. Vivace

Keyboard realisation by Colin Hand.

2. Largo

3. Allegro

SYRINX

Claude Debussy (1862-1918)

ARIA

Albert Roussel (1869-1937)

38

ALLEGRO from Sonata in C

Wolfgang Amadeus Mozart (1756-1791)

ANDANTINO from FANTASIE

Gabriel Fauré (1845-1924)

47